Where in the House is Carmen's Cleopatra?

by Rosalie Rasmussen

To Madison,
Follow your dreams!
Rosalie Rasmussen
2005

Illustrated by Marilyn Armstrong

Canadian Cataloguing in Publication Data

Rasmussen, Rosalie, 1948 -
  Where in the house is Carmen's Cleopatra?

ISBN 0-9687819-2-6

1. Turtles--Juvenile fiction. I. Armstrong, Marilyn, 1950-
II. Title.

PS8585.A823W49 2004   jC813'.6   C2004-906706-0

Printed in Canada

About the Book

Where In The House is Carmen's Cleopatra? is based on a true story about my friends, the Coates'. As soon as the turtles were brought home from school, Cleopatra developed an attitude beyond all turtle attitudes. Spot was always a docile turtle and behaved in a well mannered fashion. When Cleopatra actually went missing my imagination got the better of me and I wrote this story.

Certain facts are true. Cleopatra and Spot are red-eared Slider turtles. Dawn (Carmen) really did break her arm, Nathan (Nathanial) is a typical older brother and Wanda (Mother) had to put up with the entire chain of events.

Cleopatra was found safely and now resides with Spot in a turtle pond in my greenhouse room on Rocky Marsh Farm. In a proper pond, there have been no further incidents of unauthorized turtle travel.

DEDICATION

Dear Wanda, my friend of twenty years,
You've joined me in laughter,
You've shared in my tears.
A more precious friend, you couldn't be
You're more like family, a sister to me.

We met at Woodbadge, in 'eighty-four,
Our big start in scouting;
For our kids, we'd learn more.
Could we have been dumber? We really did try --
Remember Inspection? "What is a fly?"

We do things together, we chatter and talk.
Go camping, mow lawns
And take time to walk.
My kids are grown now, and yours close behind,
But we help each other out and lend peace of mind.

As the years go by, our friendship grows stronger
And I pray to the Lord
That our time will be longer.
You're are such a dear friend and I just want to say,
"Wanda, my friend, just stay that way!"

Rosalie

ACKNOWLEDGMENTS

Grateful appreciation goes to:

Mitch – it goes without saying (but I'll say it anyway), your love and support is as steady and undying as time itself.

The Coates' Family – you are an enduring stream of support. Thank you for sharing your lives with our family . . . and here's to many more years of friendship.

Shaun – my grammar specialist . . . if I can't find the right word, I know that only you can make one up. Thank you for your immutable support.

Sabrina – your talents are insurmountable and I respect your life decisions, whichever path you take.

Steven – you are one of a kind. Thank you for your openness and frank opinions; life would certainly be arid without them.

Michael – my quiet supporter. Thank you for encouraging my many projects and saying the right things about them.

Marilyn – your artistic talent in creating the illustrations for this book are truly appreciated. Thank you for your input.

My Readers – a special thank you to all who have read my works and have taken the time to write to me. I appreciate and deeply value your comments.

"Mommy, Mommy I have a surprise,

Hold out your hands and close your eyes!"

Carmen was excited, she talked real quick,

At times like this, her Mother felt quite sick.

Mother took a deep breath and tried to act cool,

She had to find out what Carmen had brought home from school.

"Tell me, dear Carmen, what's in the box?

Is it an elephant, a giraffe or a green haired fox?"

"Oh Mommy, that's funny", Carmen giggled a bit,

"But all those animals just wouldn't fit!

Hold out your hands Mommy, and close your eyes

And I'll give you my wonderful, beautiful surprise!"

2

Mother's fingers went tingly and her face went white,

She held out her hands, her eyes closed with fright.

Carmen was rustling around with the lid.

Mother thought, "Goodness! Did the child get a squid?"

Then silently, quietly, Mother felt in her hand

Something soft with toenails and she said, "Oh my land!

Carmen, what is it? What is your surprise?"

"It's OK Mommy, you can open your eyes!"

As Mother opened her eyes, she heard a churtle

Coming from a rather large, green, grinning turtle.

"We can't keep it, Carmen ---- we don't have a cage!

And how in the world can we find out it's age?"

4

"Please Mommy, please! Can we give her a home?

She just can't live in the world all alone!"

The turtle kept grinning and Mother started to laugh,

"At least it's quite small, it's not a giraffe."

Mother looked at Carmen wondering what to do,

And then she saw Carmen holding turtle number two.

"How many turtles have you got in there?"

Mother grew weak and sat on a chair.

"Just these two Mommy, can you hear them sing?

I promise I'll feed them and everything!"

"We have so many pets in our house,

There's the cat and the hamster, the snake and the mouse.

Then there's the dog, the fish and the bird,

The neighbors already think we're absurd.

If we keep these turtles, I'm warning you

People will think we are running a zoo!"

"I'll care for them all and love them, you'll see!"

Carmen was happy, as happy could be.

"If we keep these turtles, it would be a shame

If they went through life without even a name.

They must have names so they know who they are,

How about Jacob or Stanley or Star?"

Carmen shut her eyes and she thought and she thought,

"I'll name this one Cleopatra and this one Spot!"

"Now we must find something to put them in,

A container or something, perhaps a bin.

They must have water and lots of space.

There's got to be something around this place."

Carmen touched her eyebrow and tried hard to think,

"How about putting them in the kitchen sink?

There's two sinks together, we only need one.

Think of the room, they'd have lots of fun."

Mother said, "NO! Absolutely not!

We'll find a bucket, a pail or maybe a pot."

Then suddenly she remembered the pink tub downstairs

And sent Carmen to the basement to find it somewhere.

9

Carmen came back with the pink tub under her arm,

Cleopatra and Spot would be safe from harm.

She fussed and she decorated the tub with care,

She wanted her turtles to be real safe there.

First she placed gravel, a rock and some grass.

She added water, and the turtles last.

"Oh Cleopatra and Spot, your new home's so neat!

There's water to swim and a rock for your feet."

Carmen sat by her turtles and sang them a song,

And Mother came in and saw that something was wrong.

"Those turtles can't stay on the kitchen floor."

Carmen asked, "How about by the living room door?"

"Take them upstairs to that nook in the hall.

Set them in the corner, next to the plant by the wall."

Carmen obeyed her mother and carefully set

The turtles upstairs without getting too wet.

Her brother Nathaniel came by in a while,

Saw Carmen's new pets and couldn't help but smile.

"You must love your turtles Carmen, up here in the nook,

I see you are reading to them from your favorite book."

A little bit later, her Mom came and said,

"It's late Carmen, go take a bath and get into bed!"

Carmen went into the bathroom as quick as could be

Tripped on the rug and banged her knee.

She didn't cry even though it hurt a lot.

She had to hurry to say good night to Cleopatra and Spot.

She took off her clothes and filled the tub.

Then soaped herself up and started to scrub.

She rinsed herself off and began to dry,

That's when she slipped and started to cry.

Her mother came running as fast as could be,

She heard Carmen screaming and just had to see.

Carmen was wailing — her hair was soakin'.

Her Mother said, "Oh dear, your arm looks broken!"

She helped Carmen dress and supported her arm.

Nathaniel yelled, "Should I call in an alarm?"

16

Mother said, "No, we'll go in the car.

It will be much faster and the clinic's not far."

The house was in chaos, everyone ran around.

The car keys were missing and had to be found.

As soon as the family was out the front door,

A puddle appeared by the pink tub on the floor.

Cleopatra was annoyed, you could tell by her pout.

She hated the pink tub, and she wanted out.

Cleopatra reached high and grabbed hold of the ledge.

She pulled herself up to the slippery, pink edge.

She used all her strength and gave a great heave,

Never was a turtle so determined to leave.

Cleopatra was free, as free as could be,

There was a great big world she just had to see.

She started her journey at a very slow pace

And thought of adventures with a smile on her face.

A problem arose in the nook by the wall,

Cleopatra found the carpet was much too tall.

The tuft, although soft, got stuck on her toes,

She tripped and she fell — straight on her nose.

Now a turtle doesn't think like a boy or a girl,

Cleopatra started to panic, her mind in a whirl.

She laid there trapped, the carpet holding her feet,

She was going to give up and admit defeat.

She closed her eyes and trembled with fear,

That's when she felt something tickling her ear.

She forgot she was trapped and rolled to her side

The carpet on her toes began to slide.

She wiggled her toes and then shook her claw.

She looked with amazement when she saw

That the carpet let go and she was free once more;

But what was next to her standing on the floor?

She had never seen a creature with long brown hair,

And her instincts told her to 'be aware'

Of dangers around her so she backed away;

But the creature before her began to say,

"I'm Sassy the dog and I won't hurt you".

But Cleopatra was cautious and thought that untrue.

She backed to the wall and found a door ajar,

She was happy she didn't have to go very far.

She snuggled inside on the linen closet floor,

That's when she heard noises coming in the front door.

"My people are home", Sassy barked with joy.

Then she ran down the stairs to greet her boy.

Carmen went bounding up the stairs real fast,

She wanted to show Cleopatra and Spot her new orange cast.

She looked in the tub and what did she see?

"Cleopatra is missing!" she yelled, as loud as could be.

Mother and Nathaniel couldn't believe their ears

And raced upstairs to find Carmen in tears.

Everyone looked and searched high and low.

Where in the house did Cleopatra go?

Cleopatra was content and fell fast asleep,

She did not stir or make a peep.

Her plans were to explore the house tomorrow,

She didn't realize her people were filled with sorrow.

Early next morning, when Carmen awoke

She thought that her heart was truly broke.

She loved her Cleopatra and she loved her Spot,

And now Cleopatra was missing forever, she thought.

Mother told Carmen she must go to school,

Because missing for no reason was against the rule.

"Cleopatra's a good reason!" Carmen started to whine.

"We'll look when we get home, I'm sure she is fine!"

As soon as the house was empty once more

Cleopatra continued her journey across the floor.

The first room she entered was dusty rose and white,

It smelled like soap and didn't seem right.

She glanced around, from her turtle view

And didn't think in this room she'd have much to do.

There were great white objects beyond her reach,

She left shaking her head in search of a beach.

Cleopatra had a vision deep in her mind,

That a nice sandy beach she was certain to find.

She hated that pink tub and she wouldn't go back,

She'd find her dream beach and that was a fact.

She walked down the hall seeing what she could see,

Spotted an open door and smiled with glee.

Cautiously she approached and went through the door,

To her amazement, she couldn't see the floor.

There were books everywhere and CD's, too,

A coat in the corner, a sock and a shoe.

She stubbed her toe on a hard plastic toy,

She was really annoyed with Nathaniel the boy.

Cleopatra didn't think her beach was in here,

And all of a sudden for her life she did fear.

She shook her head as she waddled away,

And said to herself, "I'll come back here another day."

She continued her journey down the long hall,

Stopped for a rest and saw Carmens on the wall.

She spotted another door and went through it with care,

"My beach most certainly must be in there!"

She looked with astonishment at what she saw,

There wasn't a spot on the floor she could place a claw.

She climbed up a mountain of strewn about clothes.

Half way up, she banged her nose.

When she reached the top, she trembled with fear,

People noises were floating upstairs to her ear.

"I must hide as quick as can be,

I must hide so the people can't find me."

She dove into the clothes and found a shoe,

"I'll slip into this, it will have to do."

She didn't hear the family as they searched for their pet,

Because Cleopatra was about as sleepy as a turtle could get.

Carmen put some water in a little square pan,

And placed it in the hallway next to the turtle food can.

The family spent the evening searching high and low,

Where in this house could a turtle go?

In the morning, Carmen lay on her bed,

She thought Cleopatra was certainly dead.

Mother said they would find her, but that was wrong,

Because Cleopatra had been gone for so very long.

She slowly got up and started to dress,

She wished that her room wasn't such a mess.

"I'll surprise Mommy when I get home tonight,

I'll tidy it up and make it look shinny and bright."

Cleopatra opened one eye and then the other,

She couldn't hear Carmen, or her brother.

The house was silent, except for the clock;

Cleopatra moved her feet and tried to walk.

Instead she slid off the mountain of clothes,

When she reached the bottom, she stiffened and froze.

There stood Sassy, a friend without fail;

But what was that fur-ball with the super long tail?

The long-tailed fur-ball spoke with a cunning purr,

"So this is a turtle, I'm prettier than her."

Sassy introduced Cleopatra to Hugs, the cat,

But friendships are made on much more than that.

"I'm searching for a beach, could you help me, please?"

"It's out in the hall," Hugs started to tease.

"Be nice to Cleopatra," Sassy began;

But Hugs just smiled and said, "Go find it if you can."

38

Sassy wanted to help, but didn't know how,

So she said to Cleopatra, "Our people are gone now.

You must be thirsty, come have a drink;

I saw Carmen get water from the big white sink."

As the two slowly wandered out to the hall,

Hugs raced by and pushed Cleopatra into the wall.

"I think I'm thirsty," Hugs stopped by the pan;

Then she lapped up the water and away she ran.

"I'm real sorry Cleopatra," Sassy felt so sad.

"It's OK my friend, things aren't that bad.

I have things to do, my beach to find.

I'll start right now, if you don't mind."

40

So Cleopatra started her quest once more

And spotted the rooms she'd been in before.

She looked all around for something new;

Then she stopped for a rest, as turtles do.

When she came out of her shell, she was right by a room

That she hadn't seen before, it was pink and maroon.

As she wandered inside, she smelled the air.

It smelled sweet and pretty, just like the lady's hair.

She bumped into a dresser and hurt her head;

Then she spotted her beach under the bed.

She was so very happy, she thought she would burst,

And besides all that, she was dying of thirst.

Her heart was pounding deep in her chest;

But she knew right now she just couldn't rest

Until she climbed inside that big cardboard box

To a world of water and plants and rocks...

Cleopatra remembered long ago at school

That a teacher lifted Spot and her from their turtle pool.

She put them into a cardboard box like that,

Then life turned into chaos, especially with that cat!

Now a turtle can dream, just like me and you,

And Cleopatra thought her dream would come true

If she could climb into the box, she'd truly reach

Her world of dreams and her beautiful beach.

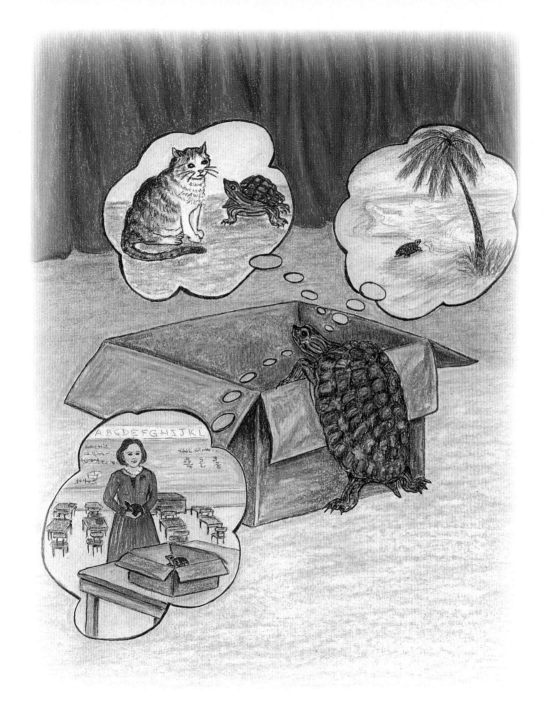

So with great effort, she climbed up the side

And was truly excited when she plopped inside.

When she reached the bottom, she looked around

And was confused when her beach was not found.

"I'll never find it, my beach is gone!"

Cleopatra couldn't understand where she had gone wrong.

But her biggest problem wasn't that fact.

The problem was...she was stuck on her back!

When the family returned home later that day,

Carmen checked the pink tub, her heart full of dismay.

"I miss Cleopatra, I miss her so much."

Then she gave Spot a loving touch.

Mother was in her bedroom changing her clothes

When out of the quiet, a noise arose.

"What is that noise?" Mother thought to herself.

"Is it a goblin, a spook or maybe an elf?"

The sound continued and Mother glanced at the bed,

"It's coming from there, or it's all in my head."

As she looked under the bed, the noise got louder;

And when she peeked in the box, she couldn't be prouder.

For there in the box with a look of disgust

Was a flailing turtle, who could do nothing but trust.

Mother broke into a smile and felt great relief;

To find Cleopatra alive was beyond belief.

48

Mother hid Cleopatra away from view;

There was something special she wanted to do.

She called for Carmen to come real quick,

And Carmen came running a-lickety-split.

"Hold out your hands, Carmen; and close your eyes

And I will give you a wonderful, beautiful surprise."

Carmen was excited and played Mother's game.

When she opened her eyes, from her mouth no words came.

"Oh Mommy, it's Cleopatra!" Carmen finally said.

"I found her in a box, right under my bed."

When Carmen took Cleopatra back to the tub,

Mother had a tear she just had to rub.

The evening was happy, Cleopatra was home;

The family wasn't searching for a turtle on the roam.

Carmen cleaned the turtle tub and gave them some food;

Everyone in the house was in a fantastic mood.

Carmen went to bed with a happy heart,

She knew she would find Cleopatra, right from the start.

In the meantime, Cleopatra developed her pout;

She hated that pink tub, and she wanted out!

In the morning, Carmen awoke from her sleep

And jumped out of bed with a flying leap.

She ran to the pink tub and what did she see?

"Cleopatra is missing!" she yelled, as loud as could be.

Mother and Nathaniel couldn't believe their ears,

They raced to the hall and found Carmen in tears.

"That turtle must have wings under her shell,"

But Mother was worried...from her eyes you could tell.

The family left the house as usual once more;

Cleopatra was on the prowl and waddled across the floor.

She would find her beach, she had no doubt;

But as she reached the landing, she heard Sassy shout,

"Look out Cleopatra, grab onto the rail!"

But Cleopatra pulled in her head, her legs and her tail.

As she rolled down the stairs, she was dizzy indeed.

She looked like a snowball quickly gathering speed.

She landed with a plunk on the living room floor,

Rolled across the carpet and lodged by the door.

She thought her brains were a scrambled mush;

Then all of a sudden, there was a silent hush.

Cleopatra awoke when the door hit her shell;

She didn't know how long it had been since she fell.

But if the family was home, evening was near

And they'd find her again, her biggest fear.

Now how could you miss a turtle stuck under a door?

As the family came in, Carmen was yelling once more,

"We've killed Cleopatra! I can't see her breath!"

But Mother was calm, even though scared to death.

"She's in her shell, let's wait awhile."

Then she went to the phone and started to dial.

Cleopatra poked out her head and her legs a bit.

Nathaniel was relieved and just had to sit.

Cleopatra tried walking but felt rather dizzy.

That's when Carmen got excited and flew in a tizzy.

Mother came back to settle things down,

And she looked at Cleopatra with a smile and a frown.

"Cleopatra's not happy living here with us,"

Before Mother could finish, Carmen started to fuss.

"Let me finish talking Carmen, it's not all that harsh,

I just finished talking to Auntie out at Rocky Marsh.

There's a turtle pool at Auntie and Uncle's farm,

There your turtles would be safe and free from harm."

Carmen stood there wondering just what to say.

"Would Spot go there too? Would we take them today?"

So out came the box, it was placed on a chair.

Cleopatra was certain her beach was in there.

The family gathered their things and went to the car,

The trip to the country wasn't very far.

They took the turtles to the greenhouse room

Carmen looked sad and full of gloom.

She placed the turtles on the edge of the pool,

Then watched them with sadness as she sat on a stool.

Then Cleopatra dove in and swam round and round.

At last her beach was truly found.

It was bigger and roomier than the last one she had;

Life was wonderful...it wasn't all bad.

She motioned to Spot to come join in the fun,

That's when Carmen's eyes started to run.

"They look so happy, I'm glad they're here.

We can visit them often, we live real near."

So every Sunday, after church school,

Carmen would visit Auntie's turtle pool.

She loved her Cleopatra and she loved her Spot;

Every time she would leave, she would whisper,

"FORGET ME NOT!!"

The Way of the North

When Bad Things Happen

Among the many letters that I receive from my readers, few have touched me as the following letter did. I would like to share this one with you:

Dear Rosalie,

I purchased "The Way of the North" and "When Bad Things Happen" at one of your book signings in Edmonton City Centre. I had primarily purchased "When Bad Things Happen: to help explain death to my daughter who is five years old. She had been trying to understand why her dog had to be put down this last summer and had even asked if she could get a shot from our doctor so that she could visit our dog.

Your book helped me go through the grieving process with her and she has since decided to wait until she dies of natural causes before seeing her dog.

She was not the only member of the family to be helped by this book. Both of may parents died of cancer. My mother died in 1988 and my father followed six years later. Until I read your book, I had not allowed myself to go through the grieving process. After all, why go through all that pain when you can deny it? Even though I puddle up every time I think of my parents, something I did not allow myself to do until now, I am at least thinking of them and am able to handle the fact that they are gone and I am an orphan. I have started laughing again, I mean really laughing, and am no longer on antidepressants.

Did your book do this all? No, but it created the chink in my armor that forced me to realize that I had to grieve and then get on with my life.

My thanks